The Magic Factory

COLD SPELL

Why not zoom out and buy Theresa Breslin's other
'Magic Factory' titles?

Trick or Treat?
Midsummer Magic

The Magic Factory

COLD SPELL

THERESA BRESLIN

OXFORD

UNIVERSITY PRESS

OXFORD
UNIVERSITY PRESS

Great Clarendon Street, Oxford OX2 6DP

Oxford University Press is a department of the University of Oxford.
It furthers the University's objective of excellence in research, scholarship,
and education by publishing worldwide in

Oxford New York

Auckland Cape Town Dar es Salaam Hong Kong Karachi
Kuala Lumpur Madrid Melbourne Mexico City Nairobi
New Delhi Shanghai Taipei Toronto

With offices in

Argentina Austria Brazil Chile Czech Republic France Greece
Guatemala Hungary Italy Japan Poland Portugal Singapore
South Korea Switzerland Thailand Turkey Ukraine Vietnam

British Library Cataloguing in Publication Data
Data available

ISBN: 978-0-19-275451-6

1 3 5 7 9 10 8 6 4 2

Printed in Great Britain by
Cox & Wyman Ltd, Reading, Berkshire

For Frances

All manner of
Super Spells
and
Powerful
Potions

Bespoke Broomsticks
by the Bogle

∞

SPECIAL DISCOUNT RATE FOR
EDUCATIONAL ESTABLISHMENTS

WE NUMBER AMONG OUR CLIENTS
THE ACADEMY OF ALCHEMISTS, AND
THE COLLEGE OF THE CRYSTAL BALL

NO ORDER TOO PECULIAR

Wand maintenance undertaken

Leaky cauldrons repaired

Crystal balls re-energized

Difficult and disobedient
dragons retrained

CONTENTS

Prince Icicle   1

The Magic Mitts   27

Beware of Sleeping Dragons!   51

Happy Hogmanay   69

Prince Icicle

'AHHHH-CHOOOOOOO!!!!!!!!!'

The stone gargoyle sitting on the windowsill at the top of the Tallest Tower of Starling Castle gave the most enormous sneeze.

'AHHH-CHOOO!' The gargoyle sneezed again.

A big gobbet of slimy stuff shot out of his nose and splatted onto one of the turrets opposite.

'Yech!' said Midden the messy little witch. She looked out of the window at the runny green goo trickling down the castle wall. 'That's *disgusting*! What's the matter with you today, Growl?'

'Sorry about that.' Growl the Gargoyle wiped his nose on the tissue Midden handed him. 'Got a shiver there.'

1

'Gargoyles are made of stone,' said Midden. 'You're not supposed to feel the cold.'

'Wind must have changed round suddenly,' said Growl.

'Oh-oh,' said Midden. 'It's not blowing from the north now, is it?'

' 'Fraid so,' said Growl. He gave another gigantic sneeze causing the flag on the castle flagpole to blow loose and land on the head of Jamie the Drawbridge Keeper who was standing twenty metres below in the courtyard.

'Oi!' shouted Jamie, looking up. 'What's going on?'

'Excuse me,' snuffled Growl. 'Had a bit of a sneeze.'

'The wind has changed round,' Midden called down to Jamie. 'It's coming from the north. And you know what that means.'

'Only too well,' said Jamie. 'Only too well. Within the next few days there will be a commotion in this Castle.'

Midden pulled her head back inside.

'Keep a good lookout,' she told Growl. 'As soon as you see anything let me know.'

'Will do,' growled Growl.

Growl the Gargoyle was one of the members of Midden's team of helpers in the Magic Factory in Starling Castle. Growl's main job was to sit on the windowsill of the Tallest Tower and report back on anything that was happening outside. Now he swung his head round to face north, opened his eyes wide, and settled down to watch.

Midden hurried across the room calling to the rest of her team.

'The wind is coming from the north,' she said, 'so you know what we must expect very soon.'

The big hairy beastie known as the Bogle clapped his four hands together and sang:

> *'If the north wind does blow,*
> *Then we will have snow!'*

'I love snow,' he said. 'Making snowmen and throwing snowballs. Then there's snow boarding, skiing, sledging, and skating. Snow is Magical Fantastical!'

'Yes, but who brings the snow?' asked Corbie the Clever Crow. He put his head on one side. 'Two people come to visit us every year at this time, can you recall who they are?'

The Bogle scratched his hairy head with one of his hands. 'Nope,' he said.

It had been a whole year since snow had fallen on Starling Castle and the Bogle did not have a very good memory.

'The King and Queen of Winter,' said Semolina the Shape Shifter. She was a very useful member of the Magic Factory team, being able to change her shape at a moment's notice. She was also kind and helpful, and now gave the Bogle the answer to Corbie's question. 'Every year, with the cold weather, the King and Queen come in their great sleigh and bring the snow. And they will ice over the pond below the castle so that the children can skate.'

'Me too,' said the Bogle. 'I love skating.'

'I am *so* looking forward to their visit,' purred Cat-Astro-Phe, who was the last member of Midden's team. She was a cat from Ancient Egypt and was used to being with kings and queens, having once been worshipped as a queen goddess herself. 'It is nice for a cat like me to be among royalty.' Cat lifted a paw and blew daintily on her claws.

While the others had been talking Midden had been busy bringing out brushes and cloths.

'We need to tidy up the Magic Factory,' she said. 'You know how white and clean and shining the King and Queen are. Our workshop will look very grubby beside them when they arrive. Let's get started.'

'Why can't we use magic to do the cleaning?' grumbled the Bogle as Midden handed him a broom. 'I've got some magic dust in my Bogle bag tucked down inside my left Bogle boot.'

'No,' said Midden firmly. 'That would be a waste of good magic. The rules decided at the Magicians' Management Meetings say that we shouldn't use magic as an excuse to be lazy. Tidying up is something that doesn't need magic.' She thrust the broom into one of the Bogle's four hands. 'Off you go, Bogle. The sooner we begin, the sooner we'll finish. Then, when the King and Queen of Winter bring the snow, we can go and play.'

'I love playing,' said the Bogle. 'It will be great fun throwing snowballs and making snowmen. Won't it, Midden?'

'It's all right for you, Bogle,' said Midden. 'You have your fur to keep you warm. When winter comes my fingers and toes will be freezing.'

'I'll knit you a nice warm scarf and a pair of socks and mitts,' said the Bogle.

'I didn't know you could knit,' said Midden to the Bogle.

'I can't,' said the Bogle. 'But I'll learn. It can't be that difficult. Can it?'

After all the cleaning was finished the Bogle went into Starling town to buy some wool. The people in the town were quite used to seeing the members of the Magic Factory team out and about, so Mrs Pattern who owned the wool shop wasn't surprised when her shop door opened and the Bogle came in.

'I'd like five balls of wool,' the Bogle told Mrs Pattern. 'I'm going to knit Midden two socks, two mitts, and one woolly scarf.'

'You are the nineteenth person that has come to buy wool today,' said Mrs Pattern. 'Winter must be on its way.'

'It is,' said the Bogle. 'Growl the Gargoyle felt the north wind begin to blow this morning so we know the King and Queen of Winter will be here very soon.'

'Well, I've not much wool left now,' said Mrs Pattern. 'Only some balls of white.' She gave the Bogle the last five balls of wool in her shop.

The Bogle was very disappointed as he trudged back up the road to Starling Castle. He loved bright colours and he had wanted to knit Midden multi-coloured socks and mitts and scarf. Plain white just wouldn't be the same.

That night in the Tallest Tower of Starling Castle the Magic Factory team sat down in front of a big log fire.

'I think everything is ready for the arrival of the King and Queen of Winter,' said Midden. 'So we can take some time off now.'

Midden liked to relax by reading, and she had found a book in the castle library that she hadn't read. She settled herself into a comfy chair and opened it up. Corbie the Clever Crow liked reading too. He wasn't so good at holding a book in his claws so he just perched on Midden's shoulder and read her book along with her. He'd gently peck her ear when he'd finished a page and was ready for her to turn over.

On the rug Semolina the Shape Shifter curled herself into one of her favourite shapes — an old cushion. Cat-Astro-Phe, the cat from Ancient Egypt, nestled close beside her to take a catnap.

Growl sat in the window gazing out to the hills in the north. He preferred being outside, but the window was always left open so that he could join in the conversation if he wanted.

So everyone was settled. Apart from the Bogle. When he sat down that night after dinner to begin knitting Midden could see that he was in a grump.

'What's the matter, Bogle?' she asked him.

The Bogle showed Midden his white wool. 'I didn't want a plain colour. I wanted to knit something in lots of *different* colours.'

'I suppose we could use a tiny drop of magic to colour the wool,' she said.

Midden took the golden key from her desk and unlocked the big cupboard beside the fire. Inside were a pair of Seven League Boots, an Invisibility Cloak, and some other things that were better locked away.

From the top shelf Midden took down the jar of magic dust. She measured some more out into the Bogle's bag that he kept stuffed down the inside of his left boot. Then she put the jar of magic dust back on the top shelf of the cupboard and locked the door.

'Choose five colours,' Midden told the Bogle.

The Bogle closed his eyes and thought for a minute. 'Pink, blue, yellow, red, and green.'

'Now sprinkle some of your magic dust, Bogle,' said Midden, 'and I'll make a spell.'

The Bogle took some magic dust in one of his hands and carefully dusted it over the balls of wool. As he did this Midden whispered:

'This magic trick we want to last
Until cold winter is well past
The five balls of white wool that now are seen
Change to Pink, Blue, Yellow, Red, and Green!'

The five balls of white wool slowly changed colour. One became rose pink, one soft blue, one pale yellow, one dull red, and the last a faded green.

'Happy now?' Midden asked him.

The Bogle looked at his five balls of wool. 'I thought that they would be brighter,' he said truthfully. 'I'll put some more magic dust on them.' He began to open up his Bogle bag.

'No, you can't do that,' said Midden. 'The magic dust would only make the colours more *active*, not brighter. Let me think. Mmmm,' she said after a moment. 'I've got an idea.'

Midden picked up the ball of pink wool. She held it close to her face and screamed.

In an instant the ball of wool turned from rose pink to a screaming shocking pink.

'Oh, I like *that*,' said the Bogle.

'I thought you might,' said Midden. 'There's enough sparkle left in the magic dust to liven the colours up if we give them some energy.'

'Would this do?' Corbie the Crow plucked one of the blue-black feathers from his chest and wafted it over the second ball of wool. The soft blue became a mysterious midnight colour.

'Marvellous!' said the Bogle.

'Let me have a try.' Cat stretched out her elegant neck and yowled at the third ball. Immediately the pale yellow colour brightened up.

'Yowling yellow!' said the Bogle.

'I could do one,' said Growl, who had been listening at the open window.

Midden held out the ball of red wool. Growl gave the most enormous roar and the red wool flashed the colour of flames.

'Roaring red!' said the Bogle. 'Only the green ball left.'

'Give that one to me,' said Semolina. 'I have an idea.' Holding the faded green ball in her hand she stretched her arm out longer and longer. Her arm became so long that it reached all the way across the room, out of the window, over the window ledge, and across to the opposite turret. Semolina held the ball of wool very close to the gooey piece of green snot that Growl had sneezed out of his nose that morning. When she brought it back in, instead of faded green the wool was now a horrible shade of slime.

'Gross!' said the Bogle happily.

'Will that do?' asked Midden.

The Bogle lined up his five balls of wool. Screaming pink. Yowling yellow. Roaring red. Beautiful blue-black. Super slimy green.

'Magical Fantastical,' said the Bogle.

The Bogle began to knit Midden her new mitts and socks. You would think that knitting would be much easier for a Bogle than for a human type of person. A Bogle has four arms. Two where humans have their arms and two more lower down near his waist. The Bogle found it very useful to have four arms. It meant that he had two pairs of hands which meant in total that he had four hands. That added up to twenty fingers.

Twenty fingers! It meant that while fastening up his boots he could scratch his head and still have a spare finger or two to pick his nose.

It meant that he was able to dress himself very quickly.

But knitting is quite a different matter. Having extra fingers didn't seem to be any good to the Bogle at all.

'Purl and plain,' muttered the Bogle. 'Plain and purl. That's what Mrs Pattern in the wool shop told me.'

The Bogle wound a loop of wool over his knitting needles, then a loop of wool under his knitting needles, then a loop through this way, then a loop through that way. He tried to follow the instructions, but big holes were appearing in his knitting followed by great clumps of stitches all bunched together. And it wasn't only trying to follow the pattern that was giving the Bogle a problem. He still had to work out a way to use the five different coloured balls of wool.

From over the top of her book Midden watched the Bogle. His face got redder and redder as his knitting became more and more tangled. Perhaps she should help him? He had worked very hard today sweeping the floors. There was one easy silent spell that she could use and the Bogle would never know about it.

Midden paused as she turned a page. Then she blinked three times and said to herself:

'*Needles click, clack, clock*
Help the Bogle knit a sock!
Please wool. Don't knot—Knit!
Help the Bogle knit a mitt!'

The Bogle smiled happily as his knitting began to take shape.

That night the weather became colder and colder. The sky grew heavy with thick white clouds. The wind shifted round and the cold north wind began to blow around the castle.

When Midden, the Bogle, Semolina, Corbie, and Cat started work in the Magic Factory Workshop the next morning they saw snowflakes drifting against the window.

'There's a tingling in the air,' said Growl. 'The King and Queen of Winter must be close by.'

Midden shivered. 'I feel it too,' she said.

'Isn't it lucky that I managed to finish your warm woolly socks and mitts in time,' said the Bogle. He handed them to Midden.

At that moment they heard the noise of sleigh bells jingling, and Growl shouted out that he could see a huge sleigh drawn by ten husky dogs coming over the castle drawbridge.

'Quickly!' cried Midden. 'Everyone downstairs!'

Midden didn't have time to put away the parcel from the Bogle as they all hurried to meet the royal visitors.

By the time the Magic Factory team reached the courtyard, Jamie, the Keeper of the Drawbridge, was standing by the silver sleigh. For the first time ever the King and Queen of Winter had brought their young son Prince Icicle on their winter journey.

The clothes of the King and Queen and the little Prince sparkled in the winter sunlight. Everything they wore was white. White robes, white boots, white gloves,

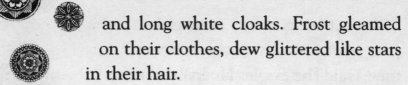

and long white cloaks. Frost gleamed
on their clothes, dew glittered like stars
in their hair.

Midden made a speech of welcome and the King and
Queen thanked her and then introduced their son,
Prince Icicle.

The Queen laughed when she spoke. It was a clear
laugh that tinkled like glass. Immediately Midden
thought of skating on silver ice beneath trees glisten-
ing with frost.

The King chuckled, and the smell
of spice and baking gingerbread filled
Starling Castle. The Bogle thought of
sledging down a steep hill with the
wind blowing in his face.

Prince Icicle stood quite still.
He said not a word.
His mother, the Queen, tutted.
His father, the King, frowned.

'Where are your manners?' Prince Icicle's
mother whispered to him.

'Speak up, boy.' The King nudged his son. 'Say hello
to the little witch Midden and the Magic Factory team.

There are not so many magicians in the world now and they need all the assistance they can get. The folks in the Magic Factory work very hard to help them.' He put his hand on his son's shoulder. 'You should shake their hands and wish them well for the Winter Festivals.'

Prince Icicle shivered.

'Would you like to go sledging?' asked the Bogle.
'There's a very good hill just below the castle wall. It's
good fun. I never fall off when I sledge there. Well,
hardly ever,' the Bogle added as he saw
Midden glance at him.

Prince Icicle shook his head.

'Would you like to skate on the ice
in the park?' Midden asked Prince
Icicle.

Prince Icicle said nothing.

'How about making snow angels?'
suggested Corbie.

Prince Icicle did not reply.

'These Magic Factory folk are being
friendly,' said the Queen. 'You should
at least say something.'

'No,' said Prince Icicle in a very frosty voice.

'Say something more,' his father, the King, ordered
sternly.

'No. Thank you,' said Prince Icicle.

Midden and the Bogle looked at each other. When
Prince Icicle spoke they felt a chill in their bones.
Semolina immediately turned herself into a snow-

person, and, high on the castle wall, even Growl shivered.

Midden looked at Prince Icicle carefully. The expression on his face looked the way she felt when she went outside in winter and forgot to put her jacket on.

'Are you cold?' she asked the Prince.

'My feet,' said Prince Icicle in a chilly voice, 'are very cold indeed. And so are my fingers.'

'You're a Prince of Winter,' said the King. 'You're *supposed* to have cold feet. I've had cold feet all my life—you don't hear me complaining, do you?'

'And a cold nose,' said the Queen.

'Exactly,' said the King.

'Your name is Prince Icicle,' said the Queen. 'What do you expect?'

'But I *hate* having cold feet and hands,' said the Prince in a small, sharp, icy voice. A great big tear slid out of his eye. It was only halfway down his cheek when it turned to a snowflake and settled on his mouth. He blew it away.

'How lovely!' exclaimed Midden.

'What is?' Prince Icicle asked her.

'Your teardrop. It changed into a snowflake. It's beautiful.'

'Do you think so?' asked the Prince.

'Why, yes! Do you know that no two snowflakes are ever the same? Every single one has a different pattern. And *you* can make snow all by yourself. That's wonderful!'

'Is it?' Prince Icicle looked much happier. 'But my feet are so cold,' he said. 'And my hands too.'

Midden reached out her hand to take one of Prince Icicle's in her own to warm it up. Then she stopped. She was still holding the soft parcel that the Bogle had given her.

Midden held up the parcel. She turned and looked at the Bogle. The Bogle nodded his head.

'It just so happens that we have brought you a present,' she said. 'The Bogle knitted them last night. A pair of woolly socks and mitts and a lovely warm scarf.'

22

Midden handed the parcel to Prince
Icicle. 'For you,' she said.

Prince Icicle opened the parcel. 'Oh!'
he cried out in joy. 'What colours!'

'The colours!' The Queen looked at the
socks and mitts knitted in stripes of roaring
red, snot green, midnight blue, screaming
pink, and yowling yellow. 'The colours,' she
repeated faintly.

'They're lovely, aren't they?' said the
Bogle.

'Yes,' agreed Prince Icicle.

The King shaded his eyes 'But perhaps
a bit too . . . too . . . colourful,' he said.

'Please may I wear these socks and
mitts?' Prince Icicle begged his parents.

The King and Queen of Winter hesitated,
because they both loved their little boy and
didn't want him to be miserable.

'But we are supposed to wear white as
we bring snow and ice,' said the Queen
of Winter.

'Yes,' said the King. 'The world cannot have Winter coming in *coloured stripes*.'

'Nobody will know,' said Corbie the Clever Crow. 'If Prince Icicle puts on the socks and pulls up his long white leather boots, and then puts the gloves inside his white fur mitts, and tucks his scarf inside the collar of his frosty cloak, then no one would see them.'

'I think that's a good idea,' said Prince Icicle.

'So do I,' said Midden, who hadn't been too sure herself about wearing socks, mitts, and a scarf made with wool coloured in roaring red, snot green, screaming pink, midnight blue, and yowling yellow.

Prince Icicle put on his new socks and mitts and wrapped the scarf around his neck. His father, the King of Winter, tucked the coloured socks firmly down into his boots. His mother, the Queen of Winter, drew his white leather gloves high above his striped mitts. They both pulled up the hood of his cloak. Inside his gloves Prince Icicle wriggled his toasty warm fingers.

Inside his boots Prince Icicle wriggled his toasty warm toes. He snuggled his chin into the cosy space in the hood of his cloak. His face had a happy glow and all that anyone could see were his pure white clothes.

Apart from round the collar of his ice-white cloak, where the edge of a brightly coloured scarf peeked out.

The Magic Mitts

'Brrrrrr!'

'Wonderful chilly weather,' said the King of Winter. He stamped his feet, and a frosted sheet of ice crackled across the courtyard of Starling Castle.

'Brrr-illiant!!' said the Bogle. He nudged Prince Icicle. 'Ask your dad to do that again and we can make a long slide to play on.'

'I'd rather you made the ice somewhere else.' Midden spoke quickly, before Prince Icicle could say anything. The little witch who ran the Magic Factory in Starling Castle turned to the King and Queen of Winter. 'Would you mind icing up the water on the pond in the Castle Park instead?' she asked them.

'It's just below the walls of the castle and it would be better for the children to slide and skate there.'

'That's no trouble at all, Midden,' said the Queen of Winter. She laughed, and tiny sparkly drops of ice fell tinkling to the ground.

'We will do it when we leave to travel on our journey to bring winter to the rest of the country,' said the King of Winter. 'I'll breathe on the water. The pond will freeze solid and the ice will become hard enough for skating.'

'Yes,' said the Queen, 'and, as our sleigh rises into the sky, I will shake out my long hair. Then it will begin to snow. Millions and millions of snowflakes will fall upon the castle, and the town, the gardens, and the park. When the children wake up tomorrow they will be able to run outside and play in lots and lots of snow.'

'Yippee!' said the Bogle.

'Thank you very much,' said Midden to the King and Queen. 'Now perhaps you would like to eat after your journey from the Frozen North? Count Countalot has prepared a special feast for you in the Castle Café.'

'Yippee!' said the Bogle again.

'Yippee!' little Prince Icicle joined in.

Midden led the King and Queen of Winter, followed by Prince Icicle, into the Castle Café.

Count Countalot rushed over to greet them.

'Your Majesties,' he said, bowing low before them, 'welcome.'

Count Countalot took them to where a great banquet had been laid out.

'Look at the lovely meal Count Countalot has made for us!' the Queen exclaimed.

When he saw the food Prince Icicle jumped up and down. He pulled off his white gloves and the coloured mitts Midden had given him earlier, stuffed them into his pockets, and clapped his hands in excitement.

The table was draped with a snowy white tablecloth decorated with pearls and silver sequins.

For starters there was creamy soup with ivory crackers.

Then, to follow, cream cheese sandwiches on pale ivory bread, and white fish with cauliflower sauce.

Dessert was a huge selection of goodies. There were trays with snowballs and rock cakes piled high upon them, dishes of iced doughnuts and crisp white pastries, and bowls of vanilla ice cream with nougat sitting on the top.

A tureen held clear lemonade where marbled fudge icefloes floated. And there were milkshakes of every variety, in tall glasses rimmed in frosted sugar.

In the centre was a special winter cake made in the shape of an enormous iceberg, with white chocolate polar bears standing round it in a circle.

Count Countalot had set places for everyone using silver cutlery and platinum plates.

'Scrumptious Yumptious!' said the Bogle reaching out all four hands towards the biggest doughnut he could see.

Midden coughed loudly and gave him a look. The Bogle drew his hands back and stuffed them in his pockets. Well, three of his hands anyway. His fourth hand he kept out, hovering near the biggest doughnut so that he would be ready to snatch it when Midden told him he was allowed to begin.

Afterwards, when even the Bogle said he'd had enough to eat, the King and Queen thanked Count Countalot.

And so did Prince Icicle.

'Now,' said the Queen. 'We would love to see round the Magic Factory. It's a whole year since we have visited you, Midden, and I'm sure you've invented lots more exciting spells and potions.'

'I, and my team of helpers, would be honoured,' said Midden.

As they walked across the Castle Courtyard the Bogle could see that the ice that the King had put down earlier was beginning to melt.

'If we want to play slides,' he whispered to Prince Icicle, 'we'll have to do it soon.'

'Can I go and play now?' Prince Icicle asked his parents.

'Later,' his father told him.

Midden led the way down the stairs to the Deepest Dungeon of the Castle. Then she opened the Hidden Door, and they all walked along the Secret Passage that came out at the Magic Factory shop. They went through to the back of the shop and climbed up and up the spiral staircase of

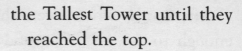

the Tallest Tower until they reached the top.

At the top of the Tallest Tower of Starling Castle was the Magic Factory. Here, Midden the little witch and her team cooked up concoctions, brewed potions, made up new spells, and mended old cauldrons and broken broomsticks for witches and wizards all over the world.

'The Bogle is expert at sorting broomsticks and making any improvements the owners might want,' said Midden, as they came into the Magic Factory workshop.

The Bogle gave a big happy smile. Although he wasn't very fond of working, he did like to be praised for any work he did.

Midden took the King and Queen to the corner where the Bogle kept the broomsticks.

'He fits stabilizers on the junior models to help the teeny tiny trainee witches and wizards. And, at

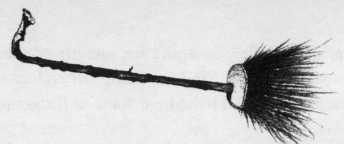

the other end of the scale, he can soup-up the more-powerful broomsticks.' Midden nudged the Bogle. 'You'd really like to show the King and Queen your new model, wouldn't you, Bogle?'

'No,' said the Bogle in a very quiet voice so that neither Midden nor the King and Queen could hear. 'What I'd really like to do is go outside and play.'

'Me too,' said Prince Icicle, who was standing close to the Bogle and had heard what he said.

Prince Icicle tugged at his mother's hand. A flurry of sleet cascaded from the sleeve of her dress. Prince Icicle blinked the drops away and looked up at his mum. 'Can I go outside and play now?'

'Later,' his mother whispered to him.

After the Bogle had shown the visitors the broomsticks he was working on, it was the turn of Corbie the Clever Crow. Corbie was good at collecting ingredients for magic. He flew near and far, sometimes even into the swamp beyond Starling Castle, to collect special herbs and flowers. He had put some of his samples on display.

'You might find these interesting,' Corbie the Crow whispered to Prince Icicle while his parents were looking at something else. 'We use them to make trick biscuits for children at Hallowe'en.'

Prince Icicle read the label on the side of the box. It said 'Burping Berries'.

'These are worth a very close look,' Corbie told the King. He winked at Prince Icicle and covered up the label with his wing.

The King of Winter put his face down, almost into the box, to look at the berries.

An enormously loud burping noise erupted from inside the box.

'Pardon *me*!' said the King, covering his mouth with his hand. 'I must have eaten too much at lunchtime.'

Prince Icicle giggled.

Cat-Astro-Phe, the cat from Ancient Egypt, gave the Queen a recipe for bleaching clothes white that had been used by the pharaohs long ago.

'I'm so verrrrry purrrleased to meet you,' purred Cat. 'It's so seldom I get a chance to meet royalty now.'

Semolina, the Shape Shifter, who was usually a puddingy kind of a shape, could change quite easily into any other shape she chose.

Now she had taken the shape of an icicle dropping down from the mantelpiece.

'This is a most beautiful icicle,' said the Queen of Winter. 'Almost as good as the ones I make every year.'

'And powerful magic,' said the King, 'that your icicle remains frozen even though it hangs above your fire.'

In a twinkling Semolina changed from the icicle to being her usual pudding shape.

'Oh, well done!' exclaimed the Queen and King together. 'We would never have guessed it was you, Semolina.'

Growl the Gargoyle sat on the windowsill, keeping lookout. He waved a claw to greet the King and Queen, and Prince Icicle.

'What a marvellous view you have from here!' said the Queen. 'You must be able to see and hear everything.'

In the distance they all heard the sound of a bell ringing.

'That's the school bell,' said Growl. 'Professor Pernickety must be allowing the children from the Multi-Story School home early today.'

'The Professor will have noticed your arrival,' Midden told the King and Queen. 'He's probably bringing the children up to the castle to watch you fly away.'

'If the children are coming can I go out and play *now*,' said Prince Icicle.

'I don't want you getting into trouble,' said the King.

'I'll go with him,' said the Bogle. 'If he's with me he won't get into any trouble.'

Midden opened her eyes wide. The Bogle and 'Trouble' usually went hand in hand.

'Remember to put your gloves on,' Prince Icicle's mother called out to him as he went off down the spiral stairs with the Bogle.

When Prince Icicle came out of the Deepest Dungeon with the Bogle the children were already in the Castle Courtyard.

Prince Icicle took his gloves from his pocket. He had two pairs. One pair, the ones his mum and dad liked him to wear, was white. The other pair was a gift from Midden and made of multi-coloured wool. These were special gloves that the Bogle had knitted, and Midden had used some magic to make the colours screaming pink, midnight blue-black, yowling yellow, roaring red, and snot green. Prince Icicle looked at his gloves. He was really only supposed to wear clothes of white or silver, but he did love his new striped mitts. It wouldn't do any harm to wear only them for a little while, would it? Prince Icicle put on his new brightly coloured mitts and stuffed his white gloves back into his pocket.

Professor Pernickety had taken his pupils to look at the enormous sleigh pulled by a dozen husky dogs. After the children had done that they tried to slide on the ice in the courtyard but it was mostly melted away. Prince Icicle could see that they were very disappointed.

While Professor Pernickety chatted to Jamie the Drawbridge Keeper, the children and Prince Icicle and the Bogle went into the Castle Gardens. They tried to have a snow fight but the small amount of snow that had fallen earlier was now slush.

The Bogle looked at Prince Icicle. '*You* can make snow,' he said.

'Not very much,' said Prince Icicle. 'I'm only just learning.'

'You made a beautiful snowflake this morning.'

'It was only *one* snowflake. Not enough for a snowman, a snowball, or a snow-*anything*.'

'I've got some magic dust left in my Bogle bag,' said the Bogle. He took his little Bogle bag out of his left boot and opened it. 'This might help.'

The Bogle completely forgot that Midden had warned him not to use any more magic dust on the mitts as it would make the colours more *active*.

Prince Icicle completely forgot that he had not put on his white gloves. That what he wore on his hands now was a pair of multi-coloured mitts.

The Bogle sprinkled some magic dust.

Prince Icicle waved his hands about.

The schoolchildren looked up into the sky.

The King and Queen of Winter had completed their tour of the Magic Factory.

'I hope the Bogle and our little Prince are enjoying themselves playing with the schoolchildren,' said the Queen.

She went with the King to the Tower window.

'You won't see them from here,' said Growl. 'They've gone into the Castle Gardens to play.'

Just as he spoke some blue-black speckles drifted onto the Gargoyle's right ear.

'What's that?' the King of Winter asked him.

'Some soot from a coal fire, I expect,' said Growl. 'Bit of a hazard when you sit on windowsills like I do. You get all sorts of things landing on your head, like people's laundry. And it's not always clean, I can tell you.'

The King and Queen laughed.

A blob of pink fluttered onto Growl's left ear.

'Blossom still left on your cherry trees?' asked the Queen of Winter.

Midden peered closely at the pink blob.

'Er . . .' she said. She glanced anxiously at Growl. 'It doesn't look *quite* like pink cherry blossom to me. And,' she added, 'those other speckles have melted away now. Soot doesn't do that, does it?'

Just at that moment a *very* large green snowflake floated down from the sky and settled gently on the end of Growl's nose.

'That piece,' gasped the Queen, 'looks like snow.'

'*Green* snow!' the King of Winter yelled. 'Green *SNOW*!'

'I never heard of such a thing!' the Queen said in a shocked voice.

Midden and Growl exchanged glances. It wasn't just green snow. It was a particular shade of green snow. Snot green.

In the distance, from the direction of the Castle Gardens, a babble of excited voices could be heard crying out to each other.

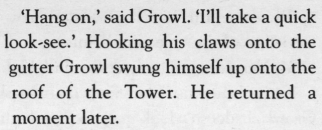

'Hang on,' said Growl. 'I'll take a quick look-see.' Hooking his claws onto the gutter Growl swung himself up onto the roof of the Tower. He returned a moment later.

'The Castle Gardens,' he said to Midden. 'Best get yourself down there. Fast like!'

Down in the Castle Gardens the children screamed in delight.

From the sky above their heads poured a torrent of coloured snow: screaming pink, midnight blue-black, yowling yellow, roaring red, and snot green.

'Pink's my favourite colour,' said one little girl. 'Can you do more pink?'

'Certainly,' said Prince Icicle. He punched his fist into the air. A huge chunk of roaring red ice thudded into the grass beside him.

'I don't think you've quite got the hang of this yet,' said the Bogle.

'Do it again!' the children begged him.

This time a block of solid snow in yowling yellow landed at his feet.

'Let's build igloos!' cried the children.

Prince Icicle made lots more snow bricks of different colours.

Then he danced about with his hands held high and a blizzard of pink and blue and red and green snow blew across the gardens.

'Can you do tartan?' the Bogle asked Prince Icicle.

'I'll give it a try.' Prince Icicle circled his arms like a windmill.

'Tartan snow!' The children shouted. 'Tartan snow!'

'Tartan snow! It's a disgrace!' the King of Winter moaned as he reached the Castle Gardens and saw what was happening. 'The shame of it.'

'We'll never hear the end of this,' the Queen of Winter said to Midden. 'His mother has been looking for an excuse to blame me for something ever since we were first married.'

'What will the neighbours think?' said the King.

'Oh my goodness!' said Midden. She suddenly thought of all the people that lived in the Frozen North.

Coloured polar bears? No white snow for Santa Claus? What about Jack Frost? It wouldn't be the same if the tree branches weren't frosted white.

'How will the reindeer find food?' said the King. 'They'll never see where the grass and moss is growing for them to eat. Not if we have *green* snow.'

'The weather forecast will no longer say "white-out",' said the Queen. 'There are going to be a lot of very confused people.'

'But happy,' said Midden. She pointed to where the children from the Multi-Story School were playing in the Castle Gardens.

They had made red snowmen, and pink snowmen, and blue-black, and green and yellow snowmen. Now they were throwing multi-coloured snowballs at each other.

Some of the smaller children were lying on the ground flapping their arms like wings and making tartan snow angels.

Little striped igloos were dotted about the Castle Gardens.

'Look how happy they are,' said Midden. 'Look how happy your son is,' she added as Prince Icicle raced past

them, closely followed by the Bogle throwing four
snowballs at the same time.

The Bogle saw Midden.

Prince Icicle saw his parents.

They screeched to a halt.

'How did this happen?' demanded the King of Winter in a stern voice.

The Bogle and Prince Icicle hung their heads.

'I'm to blame,' said the Bogle. 'The children were so upset because there was no snow. I knew that the King and Queen were busy so I asked Prince Icicle to make some.'

'It was my fault too,' said Prince Icicle bravely. 'I didn't put my white gloves over my multi-coloured ones and so the snow I made didn't come out white.'

'But it shouldn't just happen because you're wearing coloured gloves,' said the Queen.

'Bogle!' said Midden. 'Is there any magic dust left in your Bogle bag?'

'Ummm.' The Bogle shuffled his feet. 'Ummm,' he said.

'I thought so,' said Midden. She pulled her magic wand from behind her ear. Zippity Zap!!!

She waved her magic wand and the coloured snow became a magical, white, winter wonderland.

The King and Queen of Winter waited so that Prince Icicle could play until it was time for the children to go home. Then they climbed into their sleigh and prepared to leave.

The husky dogs strained on their reins. The sleigh moved forward slowly. The runners creaked on the cobblestones but it did not move.

Little Prince Icicle popped his head up from under his warm blanket.

'May I try to make some ice?'

The King exchanged a worried look with the Queen. But they both nodded.

Little Prince Icicle pointed his finger. A long strip of ice settled on the cobblestones in the Castle Courtyard.

Midden peered at it nervously. It was a faint dark bluish-black colour. Whew! she thought. At least it wasn't roaring red.

The husky dogs pulled harder, and the sleigh began to slide slowly towards the castle gate.

'On! On!' shouted the Queen of Winter.

With a hiss from its runners the sleigh moved smoothly forward.

'Faster! Faster!' cried the King of Winter.

The sleigh gathered speed. Now it was rushing under the arch and over the drawbridge.

'Fly up! Fly up!' called Prince Icicle.

The husky dogs were a blur of movement and then, like a great white swan, the sleigh rose into the air.

'Hurrah!' The watchers below gave a big cheer.

The sleigh circled round Starling Castle. The King and Queen waved down to Jamie the Drawbridge

Keeper, to Count Countalot, to Professor Pernickety and all the schoolchildren, and to Midden and her team of helpers in the Magic Factory. From the Castle Courtyard they all waved back. Then they ran to the battlements to watch.

The sleigh flew low over the pond in the Castle Park. The King leaned out and blew a blast of icy breath onto the surface of the water. Immediately it froze into rock-hard ice. Then the Queen called out an order to the huskies and they turned to head south. They were off on their journey to bring winter to the rest of the land. Just before the sleigh disappeared the Bogle saw little Prince Icicle lift his hand and wave a last farewell.

A stream of rainbow coloured snowflakes swirled out and trailed behind the departing sleigh.

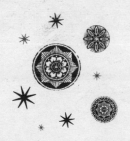

Beware of Sleeping Dragons!

'Beware of sleeping dragons!'

The Bogle was reading one of his favourite books, *Handy Hints for Would-be Witches and Wizards*, and he had reached a very interesting chapter.

It was all about dragons.

'Dragons,' the Bogle read, '*even quite friendly ones, do not like being disturbed when sleeping. If woken up, a dragon can become extremely cross. It may attack, and even attempt to eat, anyone standing nearby. Do NOT try to wake up a dragon that is asleep. They don't like it.*'

The Bogle nodded his big hairy head. He understood this perfectly. He didn't like being woken up either. He was very fond of lying in his bed, and reluctant to get out of it when morning came. During the day he loved taking short rests. But often when he was napping, Midden, the little witch who was in charge of the Magic Factory, would shake him awake. Usually because there was something she wanted him to do.

'Polish my crystal ball, Bogle, please,' Midden would say.

Or, 'The cauldron could do with a good clean out, thank you.'

Or, 'Please will you have a look at this broken broomstick and see if you can repair it?'

Or, 'Come on, Bogle,' Midden would coax him, 'the spell books have become all mixed up and need sorting out.'

The Bogle felt that it was because he had four hands that Midden gave him twice as much work as everyone else. But the Bogle needed his four hands. For instance, just now, the Bogle kept two hands holding his book steady, scratched his nose with the third, and used the last one to turn over the page. He settled himself deeper into his chair in the Magic Factory workshops in Starling Castle and read the first sentence at the top of the new page.

If handled properly, some dragons can be quite friendly.
The Bogle thought what it might be like having a dragon for a friend. Perhaps the dragon would let him sit on its back? The Bogle imagined himself riding on a dragon as it flew through the sky.

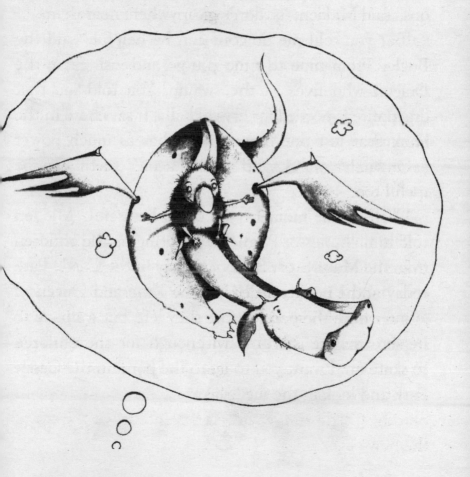

At that moment Midden came into the room. 'There you are, Bogle! I've been looking for you. What have you got there?'

Midden leaned over his shoulder and read from his book. 'Dragons!' she said. 'The best rule regarding dragons,' said Midden, 'is, don't go anywhere near them.'

'But you told me dragons can be helpful,' said the Bogle. 'From time to time you go and visit Snap the Dragon who lives in the swamp. You told me that dragonfire is needed for crystal balls. It says here in the book that just one dragon scale has as much power as a witch's wand, and that dragon's teeth can be useful too.'

'Well, at the moment *you* could be useful,' Midden told him. 'Professor Pernickety is bringing the children from the Multi-Story School to play in the Castle Park today and I need your help. The King and Queen of Winter froze the pond before they left, but we have to be sure that it is still hard enough for the children to skate on. I want you to go to the pond in the Castle Park and look at the ice.'

The Bogle groaned. What *he* wanted to do was go to the swamp not far from the castle and look for Snap the Dragon.

'Why can't one of the others go to the pond?' the Bogle asked Midden.

'Corbie and Cat are already there putting up the lanterns,' Midden told him. 'Growl has gone to help Professor Pernickety bring the children over from the Multi-Story School. Semolina has changed herself into an air pump and is blowing up balloons. And I'm collecting a big net to hold the balloons until it's time to give them to the children.'

'I was just at a good bit in my book,' grumbled the Bogle.

'Why don't you take your book with you?' suggested Midden. 'Then if there is a spare moment, you can read it. Here,' she added, fumbling in the pocket of her witch's cape, 'have a loan of my magic spectacles. That will help you see if the ice is solid all the way to the bottom of the pond.'

The Bogle took Midden's magic spectacles, stuffed his book inside his right Bogle boot, and lumbered off to the Castle Park.

He went out of the door of the Magic Factory and down the spiral staircase of the Tallest Tower. Then he went through the shop and along the Secret Passage, opened the Hidden Door, and stepped into the Deepest Dungeon. From there he climbed the stairs out to the Castle Courtyard.

As he walked over the drawbridge of Starling Castle, the Bogle thought about how close the pond in the Castle Park was to the swamp where Snap the Dragon lived. Snap was a very shy dragon, but perhaps he might catch a glimpse of him today? The Bogle decided he would keep a sharp lookout.

The Bogle put on Midden's magic spectacles. With these special spectacles everything that was far away appeared as though it were right under his nose. The Bogle could see Cat and Corbie hanging the lanterns among the trees round the pond just as if he was standing next to them.

He turned his head. He saw Growl the Gargoyle with Professor Pernickety leading the schoolchildren out of the Multi-Story School. The Bogle also saw that two children, Bad George and Rude Arabella, were lagging behind.

Bad George was the most badly behaved boy that had ever been in Professor Pernickety's Multi-Story School. Every day in the playground, instead of playing properly, he ran around pushing and shoving other children.

Rude Arabella was the rudest child that the people of Starling town had ever met. She never said 'please' or 'thank you' and was just as likely to stick her tongue out at you as say 'good morning'.

Like the Bogle, Rude Arabella and Bad George were also looking for something on their way to the pond.

Unlike the Bogle, *they* were looking for mischief.

As he trudged through the snow towards the Castle Park the Bogle was thinking again about dragons.

The oldest wizard in the world, Necromancer Nastius, had a dragon that he rode on. The Bogle knew that Snap the Dragon, who lived in the swamp near the castle, wasn't half as huge as the Necromancer's dragon. But Snap was still a very impressive dragon.

He had a long pointed tail covered in jaggy spikes, big leathery blue and green wings, and golden scales over all his body. And Snap could definitely breathe fire. The Bogle knew this, because once at a summer barbecue the Magic Factory had run out of coals. The food was not yet cooked so Corbie the Clever Crow had flown over to the swamp and asked Snap if he'd mind popping along for a minute and giving the fire a blast of his hot breath.

When the Bogle got to the pond he very carefully tried out the ice. He stamped with his big feet and peered at it closely with the magic spectacles to be absolutely sure that it was frozen all the way down. Then he waved his arms to Growl and Professor Pernickety to let them know that the ice was safe for the children to play on.

As soon as the children arrived they went on to the ice and began to slip and slide. Growl and the Bogle and Professor Pernickety skated about keeping a watchful eye on them.

The children saw Midden and Semolina coming

with the big net full of balloons. They rushed to collect a balloon and began to throw them to each other. The Bogle joined in the game. He fell over in the snow and the children began to pelt him with snowballs. He got up and ran away laughing. He didn't notice that his book *Handy Hints for Would-be Witches and Wizards* had fallen out of his Bogle boot.

But Bad George and Rude Arabella had seen it lying in the snow.

They both made a grab for the Bogle's book. 'I saw it first!' Bad George pushed Rude Arabella.

Rude Arabella pushed him back even harder. He sat down in the snow. She snatched the book from his hand.

'Oh look,' she said. 'This chapter is all about dragons! It says that a single dragon scale is as powerful as a witch's wand.'

Bad George peered over her shoulder. 'Really?' he exclaimed. 'There's a dragon lives in the swamp, just over there.'

'I knew that already,' said Rude Arabella. She flicked a page. 'This book shows you how to recognize a dragon's footprints.'

'And it's been snowing,' said Bad George.

They looked at each other.

'Let's go dragon hunting,' they said together.

Neither of them bothered to read the page that said, *DO NOT TRY TO WAKE UP A DRAGON THAT IS ASLEEP.*

It probably wouldn't have made any difference even if they had read that page because Rude Arabella and Bad George were both very disobedient children. If someone said 'do this' they just went and did the opposite. And if someone said 'don't do that' then they rushed right off and did it.

So Rude Arabella and Bad George crept away from the rest of the children and went into the swamp.

In the swamp there lurked all sorts of scary creatures: snakes, bats, unfriendly toads, and slimy things with no names. But it was so cold and the snow so deep that most of them had burrowed down for a good winter's sleep. There weren't many animal tracks about in the snow and Rude Arabella and Bad George soon found prints made by something with great big feet and long claws.

'Dragon footprints!' said Bad George.

'The dragon's cave!' said Rude Arabella, a few minutes later.

In front of them, at the entrance to his cave, Snap the Dragon lay snoring.

Snap the dragon was in a deep, deep sleep.

Bad George and Rude Arabella watched him for a minute or two.

'I'm going to see if any of his scales are loose,' said Bad George.

'I want one too.' Rude Arabella went to the dragon's

tail. She tried to prise up one of the scales.

Bad George pulled at the dragon's wings.

Neither of them noticed that one of Snap the Dragon's eyes was very slowly opening.

At the pond the Bogle was doing a new trick. He was skating on one set of hands and waving his feet and his other set of hands in the air.

'The children are having a terrific time,' said Midden.

'I know,' said Professor Pernickety. 'Not even Bad George or Rude Arabella are spoiling the fun today.' He stopped and looked round anxiously. 'Where *are* those two?'

Cat-Astro-Phe twitched her whiskers. 'I can sense a catastrophe,' she meowed.

Suddenly a deafening roar echoed round the Castle Park.

Two screaming children came racing out of the swamp, followed by a furious dragon. Fire flared out from its mouth and came pouring down its nostrils. The earth shook and its wings beat the air. There was

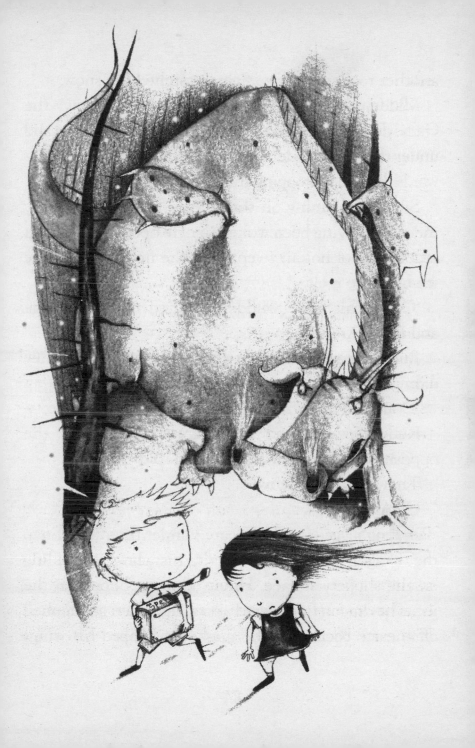

another roar and a huge flame scorched the snow.

Midden and Professor Pernickety and Growl the Gargoyle quickly herded the other children off the ice and under the trees. Rude Arabella and Bad George ran towards the pond, dropping the dragon book in their hurry.

Snap was gaining on them. And he was very angry indeed at having been woken up. He opened his mouth and a blast of hot air swept over the frozen pond. The ice began to melt.

'Come this way!' Midden shouted to Bad George and Rude Arabella.

But, of course, being two naughty children they didn't listen.

'Don't run onto the ice!' yelled Professor Pernickety.

Rude Arabella and Bad George did exactly the opposite to what their teacher had told them.

They ran onto the ice.

CRACK!

A long jagged break appeared under their feet. Snap the Dragon skidded to a halt, his claws scrabbling on the slippery surface. Holes began to appear in the ice. The dragon floundered about, and then galumphed off the ice back onto the grass. He flapped his wings and smoke belched from his nostrils.

There was another loud CRACK!

Bad George and Rude Arabella were left stranded on a piece of ice.

'Help!' shrieked Rude Arabella.

'Help!' screamed Bad George.

In her haste to gather up the children Midden had left her broomstick lying by the water's edge. She couldn't fly to rescue the children.

Very bravely, Midden ran over to where Snap was stamping up and down bellowing. She stood right in front of the dragon and spoke softly, 'O mighty dragon,' Midden began. She knew this was the best way to address a dragon, even if it was only a small dragon, or a medium sized one like Snap.

The Bogle had picked up his book and was desperately searching through it trying to find any handy hints on how to calm down a bad-tempered dragon. He found a page that said that you must always be very, very polite and respectful to a dragon.

'Be very polite!' he shouted to Midden.

'That's what I'm doing!' Midden yelled back at the Bogle. She turned to Snap and softened her voice. 'I'm so sorry to trouble you in any way—' she started again.

'And it says to apologize if you've disturbed them.' The Bogle read the next bit from the book.

'Yes!' said Midden through gritted teeth. 'I've got the message, Bogle. Thank you.' She smiled at Snap who was breathing more slowly and had smoke instead of fire pouring from his nostrils. 'Your greatness,' said Midden, 'please excuse these children for annoying you, Sir Snap. Could I possibly be allowed to rescue them?'

Snap looked at where the two children were floating on a piece of ice that was becoming smaller and smaller. 'They must ask me themselves,' he said.

'Help! Help!' cried Rude Arabella and Bad George.

'Say please,' snapped Snap.

'Pleeeeease,' yowled Arabella.

'Say it again,' said the dragon. 'And this time say it properly.'

'Please, please, please, please, *please*,' said Arabella.

'You must say it too.' The dragon pointed a long yellow claw at Bad George.

'Please, sir,' said George in his very best politest voice. 'Would you please be kind enough to allow someone to come and help us. Please.'

Midden noticed that the children's teeth were chattering with cold. 'I say please too, kindly dragon.'

'Oh, all right then,' said Snap. 'I'll do it myself.'

Flapping his wings Snap rose into the air. At once Corbie grabbed the end of the balloon net in his beak. Holding the other end Midden jumped onto her broomstick and they flew together following the dragon.

Snap swooped low over the water. He dug his claws into the seat of Bad George's trousers, lifted him up and dropped him into the net. Then Snap returned

to the ice floe. His claws snapped out and he grasped Rude Arabella by her hair and carried her safely to fall into the net.

Midden flew round on her broomstick and tied up the net. 'I'll airlift them to the hospital for a check-up at once,' she said.

By the time Midden returned Snap the Dragon was in a much better mood. He was sorry that he had melted all the ice on the pond and that the children could no longer skate. So, for the rest of the afternoon he stood quietly on the grass and allowed the children to climb up his back and slide down his tail.

Happy Hogmanay

BOOM!

Midden, the little witch, jumped in fright. 'What was *that*?' She dropped the spoon into the cauldron she was stirring and turned round.

A jagged streak of lightning stabbed across the room. Midden skipped to one side.

Crack! The lightning bolt hit the edge of the fireplace.

There was a strong smell of burning. Midden glanced down at her witch's cape. The edge was fried to a crisp.

She looked over to the other side of the Magic Factory. Billows of green and grey smoke rose up from Corbie the Crow's desk and floated across the room.

Growl the Gargoyle stuck his head in through the window. 'Everything OK in there?' he asked.

'I don't know,' said Midden, now coughing and spluttering. She ran over to Corbie's desk. 'Are you all right?' she asked him.

Corbie emerged from the clouds of smoke. His eyes were red and his bright yellow beak was covered in soot. 'I think so,' he squawked.

Little sparks of fire were beginning to catch hold of some papers lying on his desk.

'The recipe!' Cat-Astro-Phe, the cat, meowed in alarm. She stretched out a dainty paw but then pulled it back quickly. 'Save the recipe!'

'Maybe we shouldn't bother saving *that* recipe,' said Midden. But she ran back to the fireplace to get the bucket of sand kept there for emergencies.

Semolina the Shape Shifter, who was normally a puddingy kind of shape, quickly changed herself into a fire blanket. She flung herself over the papers on Corbie's desk and the flames went out at once.

'Whew!' said Corbie. He flapped his wings to clear away the smoke. 'Sorry about that.

Didn't mean to give you all such a fright.'

'No problem,' said the Bogle.

The Bogle, a big hairy four-armed beastie, was also a member of Midden's team who ran the Magic Factory. He nodded his head happily. The Bogle wasn't bothered by the lightning flash nor the smoke. He *liked* bangs and explosions. And he was also secretly glad that it had been Corbie the Clever Crow who had messed up. Usually, if things went wrong in the Magic Factory, it was the Bogle who got the blame.

Semolina changed herself back into her pudding shape and they all gathered round to see what Corbie had been working on.

'I was trying to make some magic crackers for tonight's Hogmanay Hootenanny,' he explained.

'I found a very old papyrus in the castle library,' said Cat, 'which contained a spell to help liven up parties. It was written in hieroglyphs but I managed to translate it.' She gazed at the others with her emerald green eyes and waited.

'Oh, well done,' said Midden quickly. She knew that

Cat liked to remind everyone that she had spent many years in Ancient Egypt. 'Of course you would know the language of hieroglyphs,' Midden went on, 'because you lived with the Ancient Egyptians in one of your previous lives.'

'I lived with the *Royal* Ancient Egyptians,' Cat corrected Midden. 'The Pharaohs were my personal friends.'

'And I'm sure there was nothing wrong with your translation,' said Corbie. He pointed to the piece of paper lying on his desk. 'I wonder what I did that caused the cracker to explode like that.'

'Let's have a look,' said Midden. She picked up the paper and read out:

'DON'T HAVE A DULL PARTY—MAKE EVERYTHING COME ALIVE!
Make the guests hearty
Liven up your party
Banish gloom
With a BOOM!'

'Well you got the **BOOM!** part right,' laughed Midden. 'It's a great idea to make magic crackers to liven up our New Year's Eve party tonight. But perhaps you could fix it so that when the crackers explode they do it a bit more *quietly*.'

'That's the problem with very old spells,' said Corbie. 'The words themselves are very powerful.'

'Tell me what you did,' said Midden, 'maybe I can help.'

'I wrote the words out on the inside of the shiny cracker paper,' said Corbie. 'Then I made up the cracker, saying some more magic words as I did it. But when I pulled the cracker open it nearly blew my feathers off.'

Midden studied the spell again. 'If the words here are so strong then perhaps we have to alter the spell a little. I've an idea,' she said. 'Try it again. But this time, when you write out the words on the cracker paper, don't use capital letters or bold for the word *boom*.'

Midden picked up a pen and showed Corbie. 'Instead of writing—**BOOM!** Write it like this—Boom! Now,' she said, pinning some lucky heather on to her witch's cape, 'I'm off to check up on the preparations in the courtyard.'

Midden left the Magic Factory workshop and went down the spiral staircase of the Tallest Tower and out through the shop. She walked along the Secret Passage, opened the Hidden Door and went into the Deepest Dungeon. From there she climbed the stairs to the Castle Courtyard.

'Ahhh,' Midden gasped.

In the dark of the evening the courtyard looked beautiful. Icicles hung from the windows and there was a sprinkling of snow on the turrets and roofs. Holly and ivy and branches of evergreen decorated the windowsills. Midden found Jamie the Drawbridge Keeper putting up the stage where the members of the ceilidh band would play their instruments.

'Oh, I do love Hogmanay,' said Jamie when he saw Midden approaching.

'Yes,' Midden agreed. 'The last night of the old year is always very special.'

'I'm going to play my bagpipes tonight. It will be awesome.'

'Yes,' said Midden again, but this time with less enthusiasm. She had heard Jamie playing his bagpipes, and the sound certainly was awesome. Awesome and Awful.

Midden left Jamie and went to see Count Countalot in the Castle Café. He was preparing the food for tonight's party. Happy New Year haggis, staggeringly good steak pie, and shortbread, with terrific trifle and tablet.

'The Bogle will like this,' said Midden, sampling a piece of tablet from one of the plates.

She took the napkins and the cutlery out to the courtyard and helped Jamie set out the tables and chairs. Then she placed candles and sprigs of mistletoe on each table. Midden had hardly finished when their guests began to arrive.

Goodwife MacGumboil, the old hag of the Highlands, was the first to come chugging in on her broomstick. Riding right behind her was her friend Nanny Northwind. They sat down at a table together and then waved for Wizard Tangle Wangle to join them.

Necromancer Nastius tethered his huge dragon to one of the chimneys on the roof of the Great Hall. Snap, the dragon from the swamp, flew up there to have a chat. Midden quickly jumped on her broomstick and brought them two huge basins of mince pies in case either dragon felt a little peckish and was tempted to have a nibble at one of the guests.

The Chinese Magician tethered his beautiful white unicorn in the Castle Gardens. Then the elegant Enchantress from the East glided in on her broomstick followed by a couple of Spell Doctors. After that came Doctor Distraction and her students from the College of the Crystal Ball. Among them were Boris and Cloris, the terrible twins.

A shiver shook Midden when she saw the terrible twins. 'I hope those two behave themselves tonight,' she said to Jamie.

'Yes. I've seated them next to Nanny Northwind and Goodwife MacGumboil,' Jamie replied. 'The two old witches will keep them in order.'

Midden loved music and the Bogle loved dancing, so they led off the first dance.

Jamie, who was wearing his best kilt, blew on his bagpipes.

Click, click, click, went Midden's dancing shoes.

Tramp, tramp, tramp, went the Bogle's boots.

Everyone joined in, holding hands or paws or claws.

'That was very nice,' said Nanny Northwind when it was over.

'Quite enjoyable,' said Goodwife MacGumboil.

They had a few more dances and some singing and then, as midnight approached, the musicians stopped playing and everyone sat down. The food was served and people ate and waited for the clock to strike twelve.

'This party is not very lively,' Boris said to his twin Cloris.

'As dull as a dozy dragon,' Cloris nodded in agreement.

'Maybe there will be something interesting inside the crackers.' Boris picked his up. 'Pull this with me,' he said to Cloris.

Crack!

The cracker opened and a shower of rainbow sparks and some goodies spilled out—a hat, a hooter, silly string, and a never-ending joke book.

'Not very exciting,' said Boris.

Cloris lifted her cracker and Boris pulled the other end.

Crack!

Cloris's cracker contained a hat, a hooter, silly string, and a little photograph frame. It was empty but when you spoke a person's name their image appeared.

Goodwife MacGumboil's gift was a pencil that wrote by itself and Nanny Northwind got a talking mirror.

'Very interesting,' said Goodwife MacGumboil and Nanny Northwind.

'No they're not,' Boris whispered to Cloris.

Cloris nodded. 'Boring,' she agreed.

They all put on their hats.

Suddenly Cloris noticed writing on the inside of the cracker's shiny paper.

'DON'T HAVE A DULL PARTY—MAKE EVERYTHING COME ALIVE!
Make the guests hearty
Liven up your party
Banish gloom
With a BOOM!'

'Look, Boris,' she pointed to the words. 'That's a spell, to make the cracker magical.'

'Pity it wasn't strong enough to make the whole party more lively,' said Boris.

Beside him Nanny Northwind leaned over to talk to the Enchantress from the East. On the other side of the table Goodwife MacGumboil was discussing with Necromancer Nastius the safest way to clip a dragon's toenails.

Their magic wands lay beside their plates.

Boris nudged Cloris.

Being a very junior witch and wizard the twins were not allowed to use a full strength magic wand.

Cloris slid her hand out and picked up Nanny Northwind's wand.

Boris's fingers closed round Goodwife MacGumboil's.

'I'll just give this wand a tiny wave,' whispered Boris.

'And I'll make a teeny pass with this one,' Cloris whispered back.

Bong! The Castle Clock began to sound the hour.

'Midnight is striking!' Jamie called out.

Bong! Bong! Bong! Bong! Bong! Bong!

The twins reached out the wands towards the words of the spell written on the cracker paper.

Bong! Bong! Bong! Bong!

'Happy New Year!' Midden cried out to all the guests.

'Happy New Year!' they shouted back

The Castle Clock sounded the last stroke of midnight.

Bong!

Both magic wands touched the cracker paper at the same time and at the same place. Right on top of the words, 'MAKE EVERYTHING COME ALIVE!'

BOOM!

'What was *that?*' said Midden clapping her hands over her ears.

There was a blast of air and a great mass of purple smoke went rolling round the courtyard.

It blew round the musical instruments on the stage.

The fiddle stood up. It made a bow to the bow. The bow bowed back. It leaned across the fiddle and began to play.

The drumsticks sat up.

They leaped onto the drum. They gave a noisy rat-tat-tat.

The accordion squeezed and puffed and puffed and squeezed until a moaning groaning noise came out.

Bang, bang, crash! The drums became more noisy.

Back and forth the fiddle bow raced.

In and out. The accordion music was speeding up.

Jamie's bagpipes jumped from his arms and scampered across the courtyard. Like a runaway haggis they lolloped round the castle courtyard, squealing and screeching.

Nanny Northwind looked down at her feet. 'I can't stop them tapping,' she said. Her chair shook a little.

Goodwife MacGumboil tried to sit still but found she couldn't. Her chair tipped forward violently and she shot across the table taking a plate of sandwiches with her and landed on the Chinese Magician.

Nanny Northwind's chair shook itself so hard that she fell off onto the floor.

The next minute the Chinese Magician hauled the Enchantress of the East to her feet and Necromancer Nastius grabbed Semolina's hand for a two-step. Wizard Tangle Wangle waltzed Midden on to the dance floor.

Louder and louder skirled the bagpipes.

Faster and faster whirled the dancers.

Round and round in reels. Up and down in merry jigs.

The lanterns swung to and fro. The chairs and tables danced about the courtyard.

The drums crashed and banged. Faster and faster flew the fiddle bow as the accordion played louder and louder while the bagpipes galloped round and round.

Nanny Northwind's hat came off and rocketed through the air to land on the top of Growl the Gargoyle's head. Goodwife MacGumboil hitched up her skirt. She stamped on the ground with her sturdy boots.

'Eeee-hah!' shouted Nanny Northwind.

Jamie the Drawbridge Keeper grabbed Goodwife MacGumboil by the arms and swung her in a circle. She sailed through the air and landed face down in a plate of trifle.

Midden managed to untangle herself from Wizard Tangle Wangle.

'Flippety Flop,' she said. 'Flippety Flop! This must stop!'

She pulled her magic wand from behind her ear.

Fizz!!!!

There was a spectacular CRASH! and all the musical instruments and chairs and people collapsed in a heap in the middle of the courtyard.

'I think the Hogmanay Hootenanny is over now,' said Midden.

'Is it?' said Goodwife MacGumboil licking a piece of trifle from her chin.

Nanny Northwind pulled a streamer from her hair. She nudged Goodwife MacGumboil. 'That was *way* better than our Line Dancing Class, don't you think?'

'What a way to welcome in the New Year!' exclaimed Nanny Northwind.

Midden rushed over to apologize. 'You travelled a long way to come to our Hogmanay Hootenanny,' she said, 'and it turned out to be a disaster. I'm so sorry.'

'Sorry?' said Nanny Northwind. 'What's to be sorry for?'

Midden looked round the Castle Courtyard. The Enchantress of the East had a piece of haggis in her hair and Nercromancer Nastius's cloak was torn in three places.

'It was complete chaos,' said Midden.

'Exactly,' said Goodwife MacGumboil. 'What a blast! That's the best Hogmanay Hootenanny we've been at for *ages*.'

Theresa Breslin is a Carnegie Medal-winning author whose work has appeared on radio and television. She writes books for all age groups and they have been translated into a number of languages. She lives in the middle of Scotland, a short broomstick ride away from Stirling Castle. It was while visiting Stirling Castle that Theresa noticed something strange . . . Stirling Castle is very, very like Starling Castle where the Magic Factory workshops are. So keep a sharp lookout if you ever go there . . .